For Ian Michael, who is loved by his papa
—R.K.D.

To my Dad, the best Grandpa
—K.B.

Grandpa Loves
Text copyright © 2005 by Rebecca Kai Dotlich
Illustrations copyright © 2005 by Kathryn Brown
Manufactured in China. All rights reserved.
www.harperchildrens.com

Library of Congress Cataloging-in-Publication Data
Dotlich, Rebecca Kai.
Grandpa loves / by Rebecca Kai Dotlich; illustrated by Kathryn Brown.—1st ed.
p.   cm.
Summary: Describes all the things that a grandfather likes, especiallly what he enjoys
doing with his grandchild.
ISBN 0-06-029405-1 — ISBN 0-06-029406-X (lib. bdg.)
[1. Grandfather and grandchild—Fiction.] I. Brown, Kathryn, ill. II. Title.
PZ7. D73735 Pap 2003
[E]—dc21
2002276320

Typography by Stephanie Bart-Horvath
1 2 3 4 5 6 7 8 9 10
❖
First Edition

Grandpa Loves

By Rebecca Kai Dotlich

Illustrated by Kathryn Brown

HarperCollins*Publishers*

Grandpa loves
bare feet and bagels.
Coffee with cream.
Flipping the pancakes
and mornings
with me.

Grandpa loves
parks in the springtime
when everything's green.
Stomping through puddles
and jumping
with me.

Grandpa loves
baseball and billboards.
The buzz of the bees.
Popcorn and peanuts
and being
with me.

Grandpa loves
beaches in summer.
Kites in the breeze.
Pebbles and pails
and building
with me.

Grandpa loves
rowboats and raincoats.
Tales of the sea.
Buckets and boots
and fishing
with me.

Grandpa loves
cool rambling rivers.
Napping by trees.
Backpacks and trail maps
and hiking
with me.

Grandpa loves
planting in autumn.
Raking the leaves.
Houses and hammers
and working
with me.

Grandpa loves
cookouts and sleep-outs.
Crackers and cheese.
Putting up tents
and camping
with me.

Grandpa loves
drumming and strumming.
Clapping our knees.
Tapping and tuning
and singing
with me.

Grandpa loves
sledding in winter.
Ice skates and skis.
Snowmen and snow forts
and laughing
with me.

Grandpa loves
lamplight and firelight.
Old clocks with keys.
Blankets and books
and reading
with me.

Grandpa loves
warm soup and biscuits.
A mug of hot tea.
Thick rugs and bear hugs
and snuggling
with me.